OTHER YEARLING BOOKS YOU WILL ENJOY:

YEARLING BOOKS are designed especially to entertain and enlighten young people. Patricia Reilly Giff, consultant to this series, received her bachelor's degree from Marymount College and a master's degree in history from St. John's University. She holds a Professional Diploma in Reading and a Doctorate of Humane Letters from Hofstra University. She was a teacher and reading consultant for many years, and is the author of numerous books for young readers.

FRONT PORCH STORIES

at the

ONE-ROOM SCHOOL

BY

ELEANORA E. TATE

Illustrated by Eric Velasquez

A Yearling Book

Published by
Bantam Doubleday Dell Books for Young Readers
a division of
Bantam Doubleday Dell Publishing Group, Inc.
1540 Broadway
New York, New York 10036

ISBN: 0-440-40901-2

Reprinted by arrangement
with Bantam Books for Young Readers

Printed in the United States of America

January 1994

10

OPM

To my family, who might remember the old days,
to Zack, my main squeeze,
and to the people of Canton, Missouri

IN MEMORY OF
SECOND BAPTIST CHURCH,
CANTON, MISSOURI
1895-1989

CONTENTS

PEOPLE AND PLACES

Aunt Daisy Green
Ethel Hardisen, Age 7
Margie Carson, Age 12
Matthew J. Cornelius Carson, Margie's father and
    Ethel's uncle
Alberta Carson, Margie's older sister
Momma, Margie's mother (aka Momma Luvenia Carson
    to Ethel)
Miz Spurgeon and Mr. Spurgeon, Aunt Daisy's Neighbors
Jervelle, Nervell, and Ervell Spurgeon, the Spurgeons'
    Children
Elmo and Delmo Bennett, twins, fourth graders, cousins
    of Matthew
Grandma Carson, Matthew Carson's Grandmother
Grandpa Wally Carson, Matthew Carson's Grandfather
Stella Carson, Matthew's baby sister
Ella Ewing, the Gentle Giantess
Eleanor Roosevelt
Dr. Mary McLeod Bethune
Frederick Douglass School
Lincoln School
Also: La Grange, Missouri; Quincy, Illinois; Canton,
    Missouri; Gorin, Missouri; Hannibal, Missouri;
    Des Moines, Iowa; *Iowa Bystander* Newspaper

FRONT PORCH
STORIES
at the
ONE-ROOM
SCHOOL

ONE

The One-Room School

You know how it is when it's summertime, it's just about night, you want to have some fun—but you can't think of anything at all to do?

Well, right now my life was duller than dirt. I was burning up, and I was bored. I was so bored that I was stretched out on my back on the sidewalk in front of our porch. I was trying to see how many times I could let mosquitoes bite me without slapping at them. I was *that* bored.

All the TV shows were reruns, too. I'd read every book and magazine in the whole house. There wasn't a single game I wanted to play. I didn't want to ride my bike. I couldn't even think of anything devilish to do to my cousin Ethel. She's seven, a whole five years younger than me. She lives with us, and she was bored, too. She was up to her waist in a patch of four-o'clock flowers by the porch, searching for fireflies.

Shoot! I should have gone with my older sister Alberta and Momma to that Tupperware party at Aunt Conolia's. She lived in a little house on stilts right at the edge of the Mississippi River. At least I could have sat out on her steps and watched the ferryboat take folks and cars back and forth across the river.

It was starting to get dark. It didn't feel any cooler, though. I sat up and ran into half a million big old mosquitoes flying around my head like they were checking for more spots where they could take chunks out of me. I *had* to slap at them. These were the biggest things I'd ever seen.

That gave me an idea. I tiptoed over to Ethel, who had her backside turned up in the air in the flowers.

"Help, Ethel, help! I'm bleeding!" I screamed. "I just got bit by a vampire bat!"

I fell down in the grass on top of her. "Run, Ethel, run! Arrgh! It stabbed me in the throat! They're coming from everywhere! Look out, there's one in your hair!"

Ethel screeched. She jumped out of those flowers straight up to the porch, and shot into the house to Daddy.

Got her! That's what she gets for wetting up my bed! I giggled and sat down on the steps. But in a few minutes, I was bored again.

The night sky was full of stars. It was full of bats, too. One swooped right over my head. Then something bit me hard on the shoulder. Was that a real vampire bat? I ran into the house.

Inside, Ethel was jabbering to my dad. ". . . And she said vampire bats were in my hair. And she said she got bit and had blood running down her neck. And she said—"

"Vampire bats? Naw, Ethel, Margie's pulling your leg again," Daddy said. "Were these big jokers with long, thin legs? Did they try to eat you up? Well, I call those kind of mosquitoes gallinippers. Gal-Ah-Nip-Pers. Gallinippers. They probably did look like vampire bats to you."

"Galla who? Well, look, Daddy, look at these." I showed him the big red bumps that had popped up on my shoulder. "Look what some gallathings did to me."

Daddy waved my bumps away. "Shoot, gallinippers can punch such big holes in your skin that you think they use knives and forks. I remember bites way worse than that. When I was a kid and the weather got cold, those gallinippers would drill holes through people's doors trying to get in, looking for heat and meat."

Daddy slapped at his neck and scratched his leg. "They about ate me up back then. Their great-great-great-great-and-so-on-and-so-on grandkids are after me now! But I'll fix 'em, just like I did their grandpappies."

He went to the storage room and came back with an armful of old clothes. "Let me get a good, smokey, stinky rag fire poppin'. When they get a whiff of that smoke, I bet they'll even leave the state," he said.

"Why?" Ethel asked.

"Because that smokey-rag smell was too much for them," Daddy said. He slapped again. "Maybe it smelled like little bug wings burning to them. Whatever it was, rag fires worked when I was a kid. C'mon."

We followed him outside. As soon as I stepped out the door a big gallathing stabbed me in the leg. One bit Ethel on the cheek. She slapped herself. "Ow!"

"Bad bite, huh?" I said.

"No, I hit myself too hard," she said, rubbing her face.

Daddy tore off the legs of a pair of raggedy gray overalls. "Would you go get that old tin washtub out of the shed for me?" he asked as he tore up a T-shirt.

Ethel and I found the tub in the dark shed. "Hurry up," she said, taking hold of one handle. "It's spooky in here." I took hold of the other.

I got another idea. "Ethel, how about we turn the tub upside down and you get under it?"

"So you can get on top and beat on the sides and drive me nuts? Girl, I'm not stupid."

Hurrying back, we set the tub on the sidewalk in front of Daddy. Rip! There went one of his old Sunday shirts. Scritch! There went the yellow blanket we carried dead leaves in. Pretty soon Daddy had a big pile of rags in the tub. He also threw in some of his old work socks. "To give it a little extra flavor," he explained.

"You gotta do all this to keep from getting bit by mosquitoes?" said Ethel. "Why don't we just go inside?"

"Because I don't want to be stuck up in the house on a pretty night like this," Daddy told her. "Hey, I know." He started to nod his head at me like he had a big idea. He patted his foot.

"Well?" I asked.

He wouldn't say anything. Just stood there nodding and patting and smiling.

"What, Uncle Matt?" Ethel asked.

Daddy put his fists on his hips and threw back his head.

"Storytellin' time!" he yelled. "Listen long and listen well to the millions of stories I got to tell!"

"Yeah, storytellin'!" I clapped my hands. Daddy could tell some funny stories sometimes.

Ethel looked doubtful. "What kind of fun is that?"

"Lots, my dear. When I was a kid, me and my little sister Stella, our folks, and sometimes the next-door neighbors would get together and tell stories on the front porch at home or over at the school," Daddy said. "We used to do a lot of things at the old school. It was kind of like both a community center and a school back then."

Daddy grinned and rubbed his hands together. "Storytellin' time. Man, that smoke would blow all over us. Sparks would fly up in the sky out of the tub. It'd be pitch dark everywhere, except for the sparks and the rags on fire. Talk about some fun!"

"Daddy's getting wound up now," I told Ethel. "We're liable to be up all night, like when we had that family reunion, remember, Daddy?"

"Yeah. Ethel, there must have been fifty million relatives who came back to Nutbrush for the Carson family reunion. We all went right over to the porch at the old school and talked. You conked out, Margie. I carried you home over my shoulder. You were snoring to beat the band."

"Was I there, too?" said Ethel.

"No, that was before you came," said Daddy. "And when I was a kid, we'd eat syrup sandwiches, drink Kool-Aid, and tell stories. Well, the grown folks did the telling. We kids mostly listened. They could tell all kinds of tales—funny, sad, scary. These were things that they said happened to them, or things that happened to other people. A lot of those things really happened to them, too."

Ethel shrugged. "I'd rather watch TV."

"Naw," said Daddy. "You keep watching TV and you're gonna wake up with two big TV sets sittin' on each side of your nose. No more eyes for Ethel! I didn't need a TV to have fun."

"That was because there wasn't any such thing as television in the old days," I told Ethel. "They didn't have electricity, either. That's why they had to have rag fires."

"We did, too, Miss Smarty-pants," Daddy said. He had to grin, though, because he knew I liked to tease him about when he was a kid. Seemed like a way long time ago to me.

Daddy pointed down the street. "So let's go tell some stories over at the school. You and Ethel go in and grab some crackers, peanut butter, milk, stuff like that to eat. See if there's any chocolate-chip cookies left, too."

Ethel and I went into the house. "I want strawberry milk, okay?" Ethel said. She climbed up on the counter and lifted out the box of instant strawberry malt while I got our Missouri State Fair cups and the milk. "Hey, do you think this is gonna be any fun?"

"Well, it'll be a lot more fun than counting mosquito bites." I set the food on a TV tray, and we left the house. We walked down the side of the road, kicking gravel, to the old red brick school. It was a couple of short blocks away, down near the edge of the Nutbrush City Park.

Daddy was already there. He had set the tub on the cracked concrete square in front of the school's wide steps. He lit the rags just as we got there.

"Next we plunk down here on the porch steps and let the smoke blow on us," he said when he saw us. "That'll help make the atmosphere." He grabbed the old black iron banister and set down on the second step. Then he dug into the peanut

butter, and began making cracker sandwiches. I poured the milk into cups.

I snuggled up on one side of Daddy, and Ethel snuggled up on the other.

"Where's the best place to start a story, Ethel?" Daddy asked.

"I don't know." She shrugged. "At the start?"

"Then I guess that's what I'll do. First I'll tell the story of Douglass School to you. Douglass School is where I went from first grade to eighth. It's what they call a one-room school. We all sat in one big room in there. They don't have schools like that anymore around here."

The clothes in the tub began to snap and sparkle. Yellow flames shot upward in the darkness. It almost felt like Halloween.

Daddy pointed out the plaque mounted by the door on the red brick wall. "That sign says that Douglass is over one hundred years old, and famous. It's been closed for a while. Some folks here are going to fix it up someday."

Aunt Daisy Green, my daddy's aunt—and my great-aunt—taught everything to everybody in that one big room. There were usually about fifteen kids enrolled in the whole school. Most were kin to him. Aunt Daisy is retired, of course. She lives near Douglass School in a little brown shingled house near us. She plays the piano for the senior choir at our church, Nubia Missionary Baptist.

When I smacked at a mosquito, a strand of gray smoke curled over to my nose. It smelled like scorched chocolate, burning wool, and burned rubber all at once. That's how it smelled at the family reunion, too. It wasn't a bad smell. At least not as bad as rotten fish, dead cats, sour cabbage, and dog breath.

"Aunt Daisy told me she got chased by something eight feet tall in her backyard one night," Daddy said. "Does that scare anybody too much? If it does, I won't tell it." He raised his eyebrows at me, and then at Ethel.

I shook my head. "I'm too old to be scared by stuff like that."

"Me, too," said Ethel. "I watched *Night of the Giant Maggots* on TV three times, and didn't even get scared once."

"You did that time when you watched it with me," I reminded her. "Remember how you jumped off the couch, screaming like crazy when I dropped that wiener down the back of your shirt right when all those maggots—"

"That was different," said Ethel. "I was hollering at the wiener 'cause it was slimy, not those—those things. I'm not scared of stuff on TV."

"Anyway, ladies." Daddy put an arm around each of us. "Snuggle up close, now. I don't want anything coming out of the shadows to snatch at you like that thing did with Aunt Daisy."

TWO

The Shadow

They say it's bad luck to wash clothes on Sunday, Daddy told us. Aunt Daisy knew that. But Aunt Daisy said she was trying to get her fall house-cleaning done. She had to wash those clothes, and she had to dry them outside in the sun. Clothes didn't smell clean unless they had the smell of the sun on them. So she couldn't let a good hot sunny day go to waste. Days like that didn't come around much in November in northern Missouri.

Aunt Daisy barely made it through Sunday school that morning, so eager was she to get to washing. Then she went right to work, and did suds ever fly! She washed tablecloths, curtains, rugs, blankets, sheets, dresses, doilies, couch throws, pillowcases, bath towels, cleaning rags, and even her everyday girdles. She probably would've pulled the paint off the walls and washed it, too, if she could.

Then she hung everything outside on the clothesline, and that hot sun dried them quick. By then she was ready with another load. So she pulled off the dry ones and hung up the next set. All day up and down, up and down.

When the sun went down, Aunt Daisy was still going up and down, up and down. A full fall moon rose and turned a rich cream color. Its pull felt so strong that it probably could have sucked the dew right up out of the ground, and wrung the water out of the clothes.

She paused and looked around, just about ready to give it up. Then she decided that since she was almost done, she might as well take that last dry load off the line. It was so bright, with that strong moonshine, that she could even see the shadows of the blades of grass.

Aunt Daisy noticed a shadow move to the edge of the schoolhouse. It looked like her neighbor Mr. Spurgeon. He walked around at night a lot when he was in town. She went on taking down the towels and pillowcases.

The shadow glided across the street toward her. No, it wasn't Spurgeon. This fella was too tall and moved too quick for him. She bet it was Squeak

Tucker, one of her friends. Squeak was tall, and a fast walker, too.

"Squeak," she said, "come help me get these last few pieces off the line, would you? I'll cut you a piece of some fresh-baked pie."

Well, Squeak didn't answer. Because it wasn't Squeak. She could see that now. This figure streaking toward her was even taller than Squeak, with huge shoulders and a head the size of a bucket.

By now, only the clothesline was between them. The shadow lunged at her. Aunt Daisy whirled around and shot across the yard. The figure flew after her. Aunt Daisy said she jumped onto the porch and almost tore the screen out of the door, getting inside her house. She said her heart beat against her chest so fast and so hard that she thought it was going to bounce up her throat and fly out of her mouth.

Aunt Daisy slammed the back door shut and locked it. As soon as she did, something shook the door so hard that the windows rattled.

Aunt Daisy was about stiff with fear. But not dumb. You don't get old being dumb. She slipped a butcher knife off the table, and easing forward, propped a chair against the back door. That would make it harder to open, she hoped. Then she

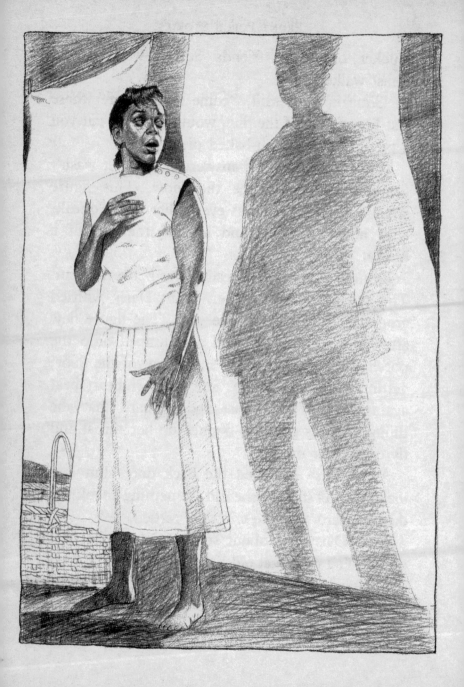

edged to the front room, locked that door, and propped a chair against it, too.

But there, in the front room, out of the corner of her eye, Aunt Daisy saw something white flutter. She eased around. The curtains! The window was open!

Aunt Daisy pressed her hand to her chest. She had to close that window quick. The curtains stopped their flutter. Everything got as still as stone. Aunt Daisy crept over to the window, just sure that something—that she couldn't see—was out there waiting to grab her through the screen. Slowly, slowly, slowly, she reached for the window.

Boom! She slammed the window shut, locked it, and snatched the curtains together.

Then a horrible sound began, right above her head. It was like someone was in the attic, stomping around in combat boots. It seemed at any minute that the boots and whoever was wearing them would crash through the ceiling. Pound! Pound! Pound! Right above her head, no matter where she moved! Aunt Daisy grabbed her Bible from the mantel, rushed into her bedroom, and flung herself into the closet.

She held on tight to her Bible. She said she held on tight to that butcher knife, too.

Well, an hour passed, then another. The stomping finally stopped, but Aunt Daisy stayed where she was in the dark, hot closet. Another hour came and went. Nothing happened. Aunt Daisy stayed in the closet all night. She didn't come out until the alarm clock went off the next morning, telling her it was time to get ready for school.

She never did see that figure again. Whatever was out there that night stayed out there.

Aunt Daisy stopped taking clothes off the line at night, you can believe that. In fact, she doesn't hang clothes outside at all. She went out the very next day and bought herself a clothes dryer.

She doesn't wash on Sundays anymore, either.

"Is that the end?" I glanced about to make sure there weren't any funny-looking shadows floating around behind me. "I like that story. It didn't scare me, though."

"Didn't scare me, either," Ethel said, squeezing up closer to Daddy.

THREE

Possum in the School

"Well, it scared Aunt Daisy," Daddy said. "And she's not too easy to scare. She's got nerves stronger than concrete."

Daddy flipped his hand back and forth fast in the air. "And talk about a lady who loved to spank! After she spanked you, she'd tell your folks to spank you, too. I got a spanking almost every week. 'Course, I was devilish, like you, Margie.

"Aunt Daisy would say, 'Matthew J. Cornelius Carson, I got my eye on you.' Then whap! Next thing you know, I'm turned up with my behind in the air, getting a spanking. One time I got a licking because she thought I let a possum get loose in school."

Daddy started to pat his foot and shake his head and go "Humph, humph, humph, humph, *humph.*"

He looked from Ethel to me. "See, it wasn't my fault! Well, not all mine. Let me tell how everything happened *that* time."

The trouble began because of a dog named Smokey, Daddy said. Smokey was a friend of Daddy's dog Rex. Rex was cross-eyed, shaggy-haired, knock-kneed, and slow. Smokey was a pointy-nosed, swaybacked, fat-bellied, bald-headed, bug-eyed, white-haired Chihuahua with a long, skinny tail. He also had an awful case of mange. Mange is a skin disease that makes a dog scratch so bad that his hair falls out.

Smokey had scratched so much over the years that he didn't have much hair on his little head, those little legs, or that stringy tail. And those few little patches of hair on the rest of him? They stayed gray and speckled with black dirt from where he rolled in the mud to relieve the itching he had everywhere else.

You put these two funny-looking dogs together out in public and you had a sight to behold. Grown folks would cross the street to get away from them.

We kids liked them, though, and they liked us. They'd follow us to school. They'd wait for us at recess, at lunch, and when school was out. Then they'd follow us back home.

Well, that fall, just before real cold weather hit, we had the worst case of gallinippers I e Big old boys, these things were, desperate and heat! My cousin Charles told me a gallinipper elbowed him away from the stove at school, trying to get closer to the heat. Some other ones tried to snatch a piece of your grandma Carson's fried chicken right out of my lunch sack.

And when those gallinippers discovered Smokey and his bare skin, they saw a walking banquet! About a hundred of them got together and tried to fly off with Smokey one time. Finally, I couldn't stand to see him keep suffering. I said we should lock him up in the school storeroom until the mosquitoes died off for the winter. Slip him in every morning, slip him out every afternoon, see. I figured that would take care of part of his problem.

Delmo Bennett, one half of the Bennett twins, offered some of his peanut butter sandwich as bait to lure Smokey into the school. See, nobody dared to touch Smokey. We were afraid we'd get dog mange, too, and *our* hair'd fall out. Otherwise we could have rubbed medicine on him a long time ago.

Well, recess came. While everybody else went outside, Elmo Bennett, the other twin, slipped into the storeroom and pushed junk out of the way to make a spot for Smokey.

Elmo and Delmo and I made up the fourth grade. They were my best friends. Guess who my best friends decided should keep Aunt Daisy busy so she wouldn't notice Smokey being slipped in? Me!

Aunt Daisy was in the back by the teeter-totters, so that's where I headed. On the way, somebody stuck out a fat foot, I tripped over it, and bam! I crashed into Aunt Daisy, knocked her on the ground, and fell on top of her.

"Matthew J. Cornelius Carson, I got my eye on you," Aunt Daisy said. She brushed the dirt and grass off her coat. She blinked her eyes at me hard with every swipe. I backed off, quick!

Well, I *had* kept her busy.

After recess, we gathered around the piano for music. Aunt Daisy's fingers pranced over the keys to "How Much Is That Doggy in the Window?"

We got to the part in the song where the dog barks. Right at that time strange noises came from inside the storeroom: Scrape, scritch, scratch!

"What's that noise?" Aunt Daisy asked. Nobody said a word. Aunt Daisy eyeballed me. I gave her a nice big grin.

We went back to singing. When we stopped at

the dog part, there came that scraping, scritching, and scratching sound again from the storeroom.

Aunt Daisy stood up.

"Wait, Aunt Daisy, that noise is probably just a bird pecking at the window," I said quick. "Want me to go look for you?"

"And the bird's probably cold and hungry, and that's why it wants to get in," Elmo added.

"Or maybe it's a dog already in, trying to get out," said Bigmouth Stella, my younger sister. She made up the third grade and sat in front of me. I poked her in the back.

Aunt Daisy looked over at the storeroom, and back to me. Then she locked eyes with me with one brow raised. I froze.

Finally, she said, "Sing, children, sing."

Well, we sang. We hit the last note, and stopped. But somebody's note kept right on going! High-pitched, fat, round dog yowls rolled out through the storeroom door.

"There *is* something in there." Aunt Daisy grabbed a broom from the corner.

"Maybe it's a radio playing someplace, or a car passing by." My little brain was going top speed. "Yeah, I expect that's what it is. Or maybe a train—"

"A what? A train?"

"ERRRRRRRRRR," low, like that, then "RRRRRROOOOO!" high, like that, rolled again through the storeroom door.

"Aha!" Aunt Daisy hopped to the storeroom and jerked open the door. When Smokey waddled out right between her legs, Aunt Daisy jumped about a mile in the air.

"A possum, a possum, a possum in the school!" she screeched. "Get your bad-luck, snaggle-toothed, grave-robbing, garbage-eating, rat-nosed self out of my school this minute!"

She started swinging that broom. Swish! She swung and missed Smokey, but knocked over the Bennett twins. Swoosh! She swung again and down went Stella.

Somebody finally thought to open the front door. Smokey shot through it.

Aunt Daisy dropped the broom and fell back against the wall. She pressed her hand against her chest, gasping.

But after she caught her breath, she went to work on me. Her lips got so tight, they looked like two red prunes. "Matthew J. Cornelius Carson, you let that possum in this school, didn't you!" She was swinging the paddle now and spitting out her words.

I said, "But . . . but . . . but . . ." And that's exactly where she put the paddle to me.

When she got through, I turned around, trying not to bawl. And what did I see? Elmo and Delmo, laughing at me! They'd got off with no spanking, see!

Or so they thought. Aunt Daisy was still so fired up over Smokey that she got mad at Elmo and Delmo for laughing. She marched them right up to her desk and paddled them, too.

Nobody else laughed after that. Well, I did. Way, way down inside.

Aunt Daisy never did connect Smokey to her possum. If she did, she never said anything to me about it. Not even to this day.

"There was always something after Smokey," Daddy said. "One time a rock bit him on his nose."

"Naw, I'm not going for that," Ethel said. "Rocks can't bite."

"The one I saw did," Daddy said. "Listen now."

FOUR

Biting Rocks and Floods

This was in the spring, Daddy began. Elmo and me and some other kids were fiddling around in the school yard by the ditch. Elmo pointed to a green rock in the mud. He said the rock had just moved. I told him he was a lie and a grunt.

Elmo hung firm. "You look real hard at that rock and you'll see it move." So I looked some more. I felt like a fool, though, waiting for a *rock* to do something.

But right then the rock did move! It twisted back and forth, and unscrewed itself out of the mud. And then something that looked like the chewed-up end of a green cigar pushed out from one end of the rock.

It was the head of a snapping turtle.

A snapping turtle can be a mean dude. It can bite a hole in a tin can any day of the year. But

it's really full of vinegar when it comes out in the spring. Wouldn't you be after being buried in a cold, wet ditch for five or six months?

The turtle pushed his little clawed feet out of his shell and scratched around in the mud. About that time the dogs flopped over to see what was up. When Smokey put his pointy nose to the turtle's shell, the turtle got still. Smokey sniffed all over the turtle's shell. Turtle stayed still. He flipped the turtle over on its back and snorted and carried on some more. Then he shoved that little pink nose in the turtle's shell. Sneezed right in the turtle's face.

That did it. Old turtle's head shot out of that shell, and snap! Bit right down into Smokey's nose. Smokey screeched and took off, with that turtle hanging to his snout. We took off after them.

It must have been some sight: Smokey in front, going lickety-, lickety-, lickety-split around and around and around with that turtle clamped to his face; Rex woofing and slobbering after *them*. And then us kids, whooping and hollering and jumping every which way after *them*!

Finally Smokey keeled over in the grass, whimpering and whining. Delmo said, "Well, the thing to do is cut off his head."

Delmo took a step toward Smokey with his scout knife in his hand. Shoooom! Smokey took off, with the turtle snapped to his face. Or maybe it was the turtle that took off, and had Smokey snapped to *his* face.

Anyway, Delmo yelled, "Not *your* head, Smokey— the turtle's!"

Smokey and the turtle skittered back to the ditch and fell into a deep puddle of water, heads- first. The turtle let loose of Smokey's nose. When it did, Smokey staggered out of the ditch and crawled under the old boarded-up AME Church. He stayed up under there the rest of the day. And howled the whole time through.

The last we saw of that turtle, he was clumping on over to the highway, headed for Canton.

"I haven't seen a turtle so mean since," Daddy said. "I think that one was washed in by a flood."

"What happened to Smokey?" I asked. I wished I could have met a dog like that.

"Oh, he got all right, and went right back to getting in trouble," Daddy said.

"What's a flood?" asked Ethel. "You said some- thing just now about a flood."

"I can tell her," I said to Daddy. "I know all about floods, Ethel. When it rains a whole lot, the water goes into the river. They put big hills of dirt called levees all around the river to keep the water in. On TV I saw pictures of policemen down around St. Louis somewhere putting bags of sand up against the levees, to try to keep the river inside its banks."

"I still don't understand," Ethel said.

"When you pour too much water in a cup, see, and it spills over the sides," Daddy said, "where does the water go?"

"On the floor," said Ethel.

"If you drink too much it goes in my bed," I giggled.

"Quit teasing, Margie. Ethel, in a flood the water covers streets, people's gardens, uproots trees, picks up cars, even buildings. When the river is really up, it isn't unusual to see refrigerators and stoves floating by in the water, houses, too."

"But we've never had floods like that around here," I added.

"Oh yes, we have," he said. "Big floods would hit Nutbrush and Canton and carry things in and out every which way. We used to have floods so bad that people would get trapped in their houses and have to climb to the roof and holler for help. Cows got swept up into trees, and folks had to cut down the trees to save them."

Daddy leaned closer and nudged me with his arm. "I know folks who woke up with fish in the bed with them."

"No, Daddy! You can tell some whoppers!" I put my hand over his mouth.

"It's the truth!" he said. "The man's name was Seemster Stroodle. He woke up with a catfish on his pillow. He and the bed and the fish floated right down the middle of Fourth Street. I've got a newspaper article to prove it."

"Show it to me." I crossed my arms and stuck my chin out at him to show I was serious.

"Have mercy," said Daddy. "Ethel, your cousin Margie is a perfect example of why Missouri is called the Show Me State. Because people got to show her everything. Margie, if I ever find that article, you'll be the first person I'll show it to."

"It's a deal." I told myself the next time I went to the library I was going to look up Nutbrush floods.

When the floods were really bad, Douglass School got flooded, too. Daddy showed us a gray line high on the brick wall. That was where the waters had come to one year.

One time the levees broke during high water while we were still in school, Daddy said. First we heard a whoosh sound, and then not five min-utes later we saw brown water come storming across the road, pour into the school yard, and cover the ground clear to the highway.

Aunt Daisy and us kids were stranded inside. The water rose up to the windows and slapped against the glass. We were all scared to pieces. Aunt Daisy herded us together in the middle of the room. She called the Sheriff's Department for help.

But then the water started to seep in under the front and back doors of the school. We set the little kids on top of their desks. My cousin Charles, who was in eighth grade, and who was the biggest, stood on Aunt Daisy's desk to pull down the ladder leading to the attic. Stella and Mary Ann, who was in first grade, were standing on her desk shaking and shivering. The Bennett twins were on their desks, too. Delmo had his lunch box in his hand.

Just then the glass in the windows popped from the pressure, and water gushed in, spilling loud with crashes and slappings to the floor. It rose two feet in the school in minutes.

Charles jumped up, trying to unlatch the attic door. He couldn't reach it. He tried again and

missed. Suddenly Charles snatched me up by one arm, swung me through the air and dropped me on his shoulders.

"YEEAAHOW!" My eyes bounced around in my head, and everything went dizzy. I wrapped my arms around Charles' head.

"Get the latch, Matt!" he hollered. I came out of my trance and stretched my left arm up to undo the latch. It was just out of reach of my fingers. I shrunk back down around his head.

"Hurry, Matt," Aunt Daisy said. "You've got to get it open."

When I looked down I saw books, papers, pencils floating in the rolling, splashing brown water. It was like a nightmare. Looking down, I got even dizzier.

"Matt!" Everybody was hollering at me. "The latch, Matt, the latch!"

But I was too scared to let go of Charles again. I was afraid I'd lose my balance and fall. By now the water stood almost level with the tops of our desks.

And then Aunt Daisy said, "Matthew J. Cornelius Carson, I got my eye on you. If you don't open that latch this minute, I'm going to climb up on Charles' shoulders myself and give you a spanking you won't ever forget."

I stood a better chance escaping from the flood than from Aunt Daisy. Cautiously, slowly, and scared, I stretched up toward that ceiling. I grabbed that latch, unhooked it with a flip of my finger, and pulled the door open. The ladder fell down with a clank.

Just then, though, I lost my balance, tipped forward, and swung face first into Charles's stomach. Everything went bouncy again. He straightened me up and set me on my feet on the desk.

Charles scrambled up the ladder and into the attic. Then his face and then both hands gaped out through the square down at us. "You, Mary Ann, Stella, quick!" He grabbed them as they stumbled up the narrow steps. The rest of the kids pressed up the stairs.

Aunt Daisy was still down there, though. She was on the phone again, trying to get help.

The attic was dusty, musty, and dark. We sat on the floor scrunched up around boxes of books and papers. It was creepy, and I was more scared than I had ever been in my life. I would hear thuds when floating desks crashed into each other. Was Aunt Daisy all right? I wished she was up here with us.

Stella was pressed up against me. She was barely breathing. I'll never forget how she shivered and shook, like a frightened baby sparrow I caught one time and had held in my hands.

"Matt," she whispered, "are we gonna die?"

I looked down at her, and I couldn't tell her a thing. But just then Aunt Daisy's gray head popped up through the opening. She sat down by Stella and told the rest of us to move in closer. "Don't worry, children," she said. "It'll be all right. God's hands built our school, and God's hands are gonna take care of us. I phoned Sheriff Stark and he told me he was sending out four boats for us. They'll be here any minute. It'll be all right."

And then she turned to me. "We were also in the good hands of Matthew and Charles. You two are heroes."

Everybody clapped for me and Charles. In about half an hour, the sheriff and the boats arrived. They carried all of us through the water to the boats. They took us over to the emergency shelter set up in the Christian Church on the dry side of town. All our folks were there, and man, were we all ever glad to see them.

"Geez, what an exciting story!" My mouth hung open. "Did all that stuff really happen to you?"

"Sure did," said Daddy. "So what did I need a TV for?"

FIVE

School News

"Folks always said that gophers were the cause of the floods," Daddy told us.

I laughed. "How? Did they bite holes in the sandbags?"

"You're close. They made their dens in the levees, so they could be on dry, high ground, too. But when the water got too high, the water seeped into the holes and made the levees so weak that they fell apart."

"What happened to the gophers?" Ethel asked.

"I think they moved to Kansas City," Daddy said.

"This old school has been through a lot," Daddy went on. "It had been a school for Black kids to go to a long, long time ago. The White kids went to Nutbrush Public School. The law back then said Black kids and White kids had to go to separate schools."

I was confused. "Why?"

"Because some folks thought Black folks weren't as good as White folks," Daddy explained. "They tried to have it so that Whites got the best of everything. They called Black people second-class citizens.

"That was why so much of what people did back then was separated by race all over the United States. We Black folks just went ahead and did what we had to do. We didn't do bad, either. Some other folks with some common sense came along and changed those stupid laws, all over the country, but not all at once. The kids in Nutbrush, Black and White, were sent to Nutbrush Elementary School. Douglass School closed down, and Aunt Daisy retired.

"And did I ever miss going to school at Douglass! At Douglass I could keep up with who was doing what when and where. Like who got sent to the corner for being bad, who had to stay in for recess, who got an A. I could keep an eye on Stella, too. We had such small classes that Aunt Daisy was able to spend a lot of time with everybody. Anybody who had problems got help. It didn't take long, though, for me to get to like the new school."

"But Uncle Matt, didn't you ever get bored, with no TV?" Ethel asked.

"Well, not until I had a chance to watch Zorro and the Cisco Kid," said Daddy, "and then I started crying around for a TV, too. But that's another story. We had a lot of plays and programs at school and in church. In fact, Douglass and our church, Nubia Missionary Baptist, had programs all the time. They were the centers for almost everything we did.

"The closing exercises Douglass held every May was the biggest school program. One year our theme was 'Hands Across the Continent.' Each of us had to memorize something about famous Black people and say a quote from them. Mine was about Dr. George Washington Carver, the inventor and scientist, born down there in Diamond Grove, Missouri. The older kids were also in a play called *Be Careful What You Say*. It was supposed to teach you not to gossip. It didn't, of course.

"Our school choir sang 'Come and Partake of Our Welcome Cake,' 'The Star-Spangled Banner,' and 'Lift Every Voice and Sing.' The superintendent of schools was there, and all our folks. Cousin Charles and Betty Jean graduated from eighth grade. They wore caps and gowns and got diplomas."

Daddy stopped, and laughed. "Well, Charles almost didn't get his. I was sitting in the front row, see, and I had my favorite cat's-eye aggie in my hand. That's a marble. I used it for good luck when I gave my speech.

"It popped right out of my hand—an accident, Margie, I swear—and rolled up to Charles' feet just as the superintendent spoke his name. Charles didn't know whether to grab the marble or take the diploma. So he slapped his foot on the marble. When ole Charles started to walk, he tripped on the marble and went flat on his face. Talk about a guy being embarrassed! And then mad!

"The next day Charles put the word out that whoever owned that marble was in big trouble. This is how he put the word out: He crushed that marble to pieces under his big steel-heeled motorcycle boot. He said its owner would get the same treatment. You can believe that was one marble I never tried to claim."

"I wouldn't have, either," said Ethel.

We munched on crackers and slurped our milk while he talked about some other stuff. The gallinippers weren't nearly as bad as they had been. Maybe that smoke was working.

"Ethel, we went to the movies a lot," Daddy said. "We had radios. We had our neighbors Leo and Laura Jean, too. They'd drink too much beer, and then they'd get into some of the biggest fights on Saturday night you ever saw, and roll across the alley into our backyard. Watching them was like going to the movies and listening to the radio at the same time.

"Thinking back on it, I guess they were always too tipsy to really hurt each other," he said. "But I told myself I'd never take a drop of alcohol if it was going to pickle my brains like that. And I haven't.

"One Saturday night Leo and Laura Jean got to pushing at each other. Stella and I were at the kitchen window, watching them. She'd push at him, then he'd push at her. He pushed, she pushed, and bam! Leo landed in Mom's begonias.

"Laura Jean left him sitting there with his eyes rolling around in his head. She went strutting back through our yard, proud of herself. Then *she* fell into the ditch that the plumbers had dug for pipe.

"She was hollering, 'Lemme out! Help! Leo, somebody, Miz Carson, come get me! I've fallen and I can't get up!'

"All I could see was one leg and one foot shooting up out of that hole. Leo crawled over to the

ditch on his hands and knees. He tried to pull Laura Jean out by the leg. He had her halfway out when something happened—I don't know what—but he fell in, too.

"So both of them were screeching for help. They got quiet after a while. We tiptoed out there with a flashlight and peeked in. They were sound asleep, snoring to beat the band. We left them down there, too. The next day plumbers almost laid pipe over them."

"Was that a true story?" I asked. Daddy nodded. "Boy, I wish we had some neighbors like that. Miz Moten just weeds her garden."

Just then I remembered Aunt Daisy's shadow. "And there's no such thing as weird shadows, or ghosts, except for Casper and Ghostbusters, huh, Daddy?"

"Well, I don't know about ghosts, but your great-grandmother Carson used to tell me she could see spirits and visions. She said she saw my great-grandpa Wally alive." Daddy paused. "After they'd buried him."

SIX

The Light

As far back as I could remember, Grandpa Wally always slept on the couch at night in the front room of their home, Daddy said. The front room was their living room. Grandma slept in the bed in their bedroom, which they called the back room.

Nobody slept on Grandpa's couch at night without his permission. You could sit on it during the day, but if you so much as even rumpled up the spread, you'd better smooth it out. You knew you better not even think about laying a dirty foot, hand, or shoe upon neither spread nor couch, day or night.

Grandpa Wally didn't do much regular talk, but he was one heck of a storyteller. He could tell some stories that would go way back and scare you so that your ears would wrap around your head. When Stella and I came over, though, he'd usually go out to the coal shed. He said being in the house with us was like being in the barn with a herd of Missouri mules. He was okay, though. He liked to give us animal crackers and Popsicles.

Well, in the middle of December Grandpa Wally caught pneumonia. He got sicker and sicker. He reached the point where he stayed on the couch most of the time. But he wouldn't go to the hospital. He said he'd die for sure in there. He hung on through the winter, and then he passed away in the spring, just after Easter.

On the day of the funeral it rained and it rained and it rained. In the cemetery my shoes got so full of mud that I could barely lift them up to take a step, or even slide them in the grass to clean them off. But we were all dragging. It was a sad time.

The rain stopped when they lowered his casket into the ground. Then the sun came out and we saw a rainbow. That made us feel a little better.

We brought Grandma to her home. They lived right around the corner from here. Grandpa Wally had been a schoolteacher here at Douglass, long before Aunt Daisy came. His portrait hung right back there in the hallway. It might still be in there.

Now in those days, after a funeral everybody would come over to the house of the dead person's

family, eat dinner, and sit up and talk with whoever was still living. So that's what we did.

It was so late when everybody else went home
that we decided to sleep at Grandma's that night.
Stella and me did that a lot, anyway.

Mom and Dad unfolded a cot in the hallway.
Grandma put Stella and me on Grandpa Wally's
couch. We fell right off to sleep.

The way Grandma told the story, something
woke her up. Or maybe she never did go to sleep.
Anyway, she said she had this strong feeling that
she was supposed to go into the front room, where
we were.

Grandma got up and went to the doorway. She
looked over to where we slept on the couch.

There, in the pitch black, was a bright light
about the size of her fist, floating in the air above
our heads. It hung there, she said, then it slowly
moved to the other end of the couch to our feet.
Then it floated back.

That light couldn't have come from outside because the curtains were closed tight over the windows. It couldn't have been a reflection from
anything inside—there was only one mirror in the
room. It had been covered with a white cloth for
three days, since Grandpa Wally died.

Why was it covered? Well, in the old days, they

hung white sheets over the mirrors when people died so if you happened to look in the mirror you wouldn't see the spirit of the newly dead looking back at you. Grandpa Wally's portrait at school was covered, too.

Grandma said that light danced back and forth, back and forth, over our heads. We slept right on, not knowing a thing. The room was still as stone, except for our breathing.

Grandma said she finally took a deep breath and opened her mouth.

"Wally, the grandkids are sleeping on your couch, and I hope it's all right," she said to the light. "You're supposed to rest in peace somewhere else now. Everything's all right. You're in God's arms now. You go on where you belong and rest in peace. I'll talk to you later."

The light disappeared.

Grandma stayed in the doorway watching over Stella and me until the sun came up. She decided that the light was Grandpa Wally's spirit, come back to sleep on his couch.

"Now you tell me what you think that light was," said Daddy.

"Maybe you guys were reading in bed with a flash-light?" I shivered. That was another scary story.

"Or maybe it was a lightning bug," Ethel said.

"Well, for the light to move, we'd have had to move, too," Daddy reminded me. "Grandma said we didn't budge. As for the lightning bug, when was the last time you saw one so early in the spring?"

"I forgot about that," said Ethel. "Well, I bet you never touched that couch again, huh?"

"I slept on that couch for years and years after Grandpa Wally died, and never got scared," he said. "Grandma didn't tell me that story until after I was grown, and by then she'd sold the couch."

The way Daddy figured it, that light might really have been the spirit of Grandpa Wally, but come back to keep Daddy's muddy shoes off the couch.

SEVEN

Ghosts Galore

White lights sparkled up from the fire and disappeared into the darkness. Or was one of them the spirit of Grandpa Wally? Then I thought I saw a strange shadow by the walnut tree in our yard, just about where I'd been stretched out in the grass. I told myself it was just the walnut tree's shadows. But you know what? I sure didn't plan to go back through all that dark anytime soon. At least not by myself.

When Daddy poked me, I jumped. "Well, what do you think about that story?" he asked.

"Didn't scare me that much." I tried not to look across the street into our yard.

"I think it was too scary." Ethel wrapped her hands around Daddy's arm. "Talk about something else."

But I just had to ask another question about

ghosts. "Daddy, just out of curiosity, what about that thing you said Aunt Daisy saw. What was it really?"

"At first she thought it was my dad playing a trick on her," he said. "She thought he had put me on his shoulders, and then wrapped a coat around me to make us look like we were a giant. But it wasn't us."

"It never did come back, did it? I mean, you didn't ever see it, did you?" I sneaked another quick look across the street, but I didn't see anything unusual.

Daddy shook his head. "No, but out here at midnight only three short blocks from Ole Man River, you're liable to see anything. Or anything's liable to see you. I heard that the ghosts of outlaws, cowboys, riverboat gamblers and pirates, pioneers and Civil War soldiers from both sides of the fence used to hang out around the Mississippi River here in the old days. And might still be walking around now.

"Grandpa Wally used to tell me stories about slaves running away to freedom by taking rafts up the Mississippi around here, too. Some of them died trying to get over to the freedom side, to Illinois and Iowa. They drowned. The ghosts of the ones who died would show the way to freedom to the slaves still living and trying to get out."

He stood up and stretched. "Time-out. I need to get some more rags and rev up this fire one last time. I'm going to the house. Ladies, do you want to come with me?"

I said we'd wait. But as soon as Daddy left, Ethel jumped up and ran after him.

"Hey!" I yelled, but she was gone.

Left alone. Well, I wasn't going to let her think I was scared. I'd just fix some more sandwiches and not be worried one bit. All that stuff Daddy was talking about was make-believe, anyway.

I picked up the knife and dipped a bladeful of peanut butter out of the jar. But I clutched that knife so tight that I let the peanut butter slide off. It plopped onto my foot.

An owl hooted from somewhere. Daddy once said that a screech owl hooting was a sign of death. So did somebody just die? Was that their ghost I saw flit around the corner of the church just then? Or was it an old ghost from way before?

No. I sat back, relieved. It was only the reflection of headlights on one of the church windows, from a truck going past on the highway behind the school.

That reminded me of a story Daddy said Grandpa Wally told him about a funeral held at some church for a mean, mean, mean old man. The casket set at the front of the church where everybody could see it clear. The church was crammed, too. Everybody in town wanted proof with their own eyes that this mean old man was finally, absolutely, positively dead and couldn't bother anybody anymore.

Right at the end of the funeral an awful storm came up. While the preacher was praying, a clap of thunder hit. A huge streak of orange-and-blue lightning raced across the sky, then streaked into the church and turned the air blue. Everybody froze. Then another bolt struck the casket. The lid of the casket flew open, and the dead man sat straight up.

Everybody tore out of that church with the preacher in the lead.

Grandpa Wally told Daddy that this church closed down not too long after that. I'm sure glad I wasn't there.

I thumped myself in the head with my knuckles. Why in the world did I have to be thinking about ghosts, and all by myself like this? I started to fix cracker sandwiches left and right, trying not to think about ghosts.

The next time I looked up, I saw to my left that a large yellow light was glowing near the river. It seemed to be slowly moving in my direction. Something else Daddy once told me popped into my head. He said that a man had hung himself from a tree a long time ago not too far from here. Some fishermen came upon the man the next day. They found a lantern still lit on the ground beneath his dangling body.

Just then I realized how still everything was. And dark. You know how the hair on your arms goes straight when goose bumps come on them? And how you start to feel hot, like you're waiting for something evil to happen? Like how you're waiting for the monster to jump out of the shadows when you're watching a horror show on TV?

Well, that's how I felt.

"TOOOOOOT!"

I dropped another glob of peanut butter. Then I breathed another sigh of relief. The light and the noise came from a barge moving downstream.

Seemed like stuff that wasn't supposed to be moving all of a sudden was. It sure wasn't boring tonight anymore!

Clunk, clunk, clunk. Something landed right beside me, and it wasn't peanut butter. With my knife still in one hand and a cracker in the other, I shot off that porch and ducked down by the steps.

"Gotcha!" Ethel shouted above me. "Those were just walnuts we threw." She picked one up and tossed it down at me.

"Girl, that wasn't funny," I shouted. I climbed back up on the porch. "Daddy, why'd you have to do that? I wasn't scared, Ethel. I was just concentrating on fixing food."

"Sorry, Bitty Bit," Daddy said. "I thought you saw us coming back."

"I wasn't looking for you guys. I was busy." I tried to act like I was normal, but my heart was thumping so hard, I could barely breathe.

"I still gotcha," said Ethel. "Now you know how I feel when you scare me."

"Well, okay. Maybe I was a little scared," I told her. "But now I know how Aunt Daisy felt when that thing got after her, too."

"Let's not talk about scary stuff anymore," Ethel said. "Uncle Matt, how come we can't eat these walnuts?"

"I was always told that the nuts from most of these trees weren't any good," Daddy said, "but maybe that was just an old saying. Most kids I knew didn't *eat* walnuts. We *threw* them! We had some fine walnut wars, all over town.

"And listen to this: Aunt Daisy was even in a walnut war once. Of course, she used some of her own ammunition."

EIGHT

The Walnut Wars

First off, Nutbrush got its name because it had a million nut trees—oak trees, buckeye trees, walnut trees, Daddy said.

There was a walnut tree in the school yard, too. This tree was part of a tree house. This particular tree house was a modern piece of architecture to us. The tree had a slide attached to one side. The slide steps took you up into the tree house, and when you got ready to come down, you could slide, or take the steps back down. The slide sat on a wide wooden platform about three feet high around the trunk, where you could sit.

The tree house was made of wood and set about ten feet up in the forks of the main branches. It was big enough for three grown-ups or four kids to sit comfortably in it. Aunt Daisy kept it locked up most of the time. That way hobos couldn't sleep in it. She let Stella and me play in it sometimes on weekends or after school. We could be in there and even look over onto the Spurgeons', our neighbors, front porch.

Miz Spurgeon and Mr. Spurgeon and their ugly kids Jervelle, Nervell, and Ervell lived in Nutbrush only in the summers. Before they'd leave they'd throw walnuts at us from their yard and call us names. We'd throw walnuts back and call them names, too. It was fun. Aunt Daisy would fuss at them and get after us. Miz Spurgeon would shake her fist at us and then fuss at her kids. In the late fall, around October or November, they'd move down to Arkansas or Mississippi. They never did go to school here. They just fought with us and everybody all over town.

The walnut tree in the Spurgeons' yard didn't have a tree house. One time Aunt Daisy let the Spurgeon kids play in her tree house. They got in there and tried to tear it up. She banned them from the place after that. Miz Spurgeon claimed her kids wouldn't ever do any such thing. Aunt Daisy knew better than to believe that.

People said Aunt Daisy actually had the tree house built for herself. See, the dirt levees put up by the town to protect itself from floods blocked Aunt Daisy's view of the Mississippi from her own front porch. She loved that old river and missed seeing it. But in that tree house she could sit up high all summer till nightfall, watching the barges and boats pass Nutbrush, just like always.

One afternoon Jervelle Spurgeon and her ugly brother Nervell came out into their yard. Jervelle had her baboon-faced baby brother Ervell on her hip. Jervelle and I were about the same age as you, Margie, when this happened.

So, Stella and I were in the tree house. I don't know how it got started. Maybe Stella said something. Maybe Nervell did. But I do remember them calling us names: "Lookit the monkeys! Chimpanzees, throw 'em some bananas!"

Nervell threw a walnut at me. It hit the side of the tree house.

"Keep aknockin' but you can't come in!" Stella yelled. A walnut whizzed by her head.

"Monkey wanna banana! Monkey wanna banana!" Jervelle shrieked. She threw a walnut at me, but I ducked. Ervell was swinging around on her hip.

When I leaned back to take aim at Jervelle's head, she slung Ervell around to the front of her. "Don't you hit this baby! Do, I'll tell my momma and she'll put the sheriff on you!"

Jervelle threw another walnut. Bam! It hit me

on the crazy bone. Man, I about died with the pain. But buddy, when I got up from rolling around on the floor, I declared war.

I grabbed a couple of walnuts and peered through a knothole in the wall of the tree house. Jervelle had her behind turned up to me, collecting more fire power. Ervell hung upside down under her arm.

I stood up, took aim, and flung that walnut at her. It caught her hard on the back of her knee. Jervelle screeched and jumped ten feet in the air. I shot off another walnut, but Jervelle saw it coming. She flung Ervell around in front of her again. The walnut grazed his foot. Jervelle and Ervell let out screams like they'd both been blown up by a bomb.

"Now you done it! You hit the baby!" Jervelle shouted. "I'm gettin' my momma on you!" They ran back into their house, screaming and yelling.

Stella and I shot down out of that tree house, and ran to Aunt Daisy's. We told her the whole story. The truth, too! And what'd we do that for?

Oh, she got so mad over us throwing walnuts that she couldn't figure out whether to paddle me first, or Stella. So right then she didn't paddle either one of us.

But did she ever fuss! She'd walk to the living room window, looking for the Spurgeons, and fuss. Yakkety, yakkety, yak! Then go to the kitchen and look out the back door, and fuss. Yakkety, yakkety, yak! Then she'd come back in and start all over again.

Finally she picked up a bowl and a small sack of white potatoes and a paring knife, and left the house. She climbed up the slide steps and went into the tree house. We saw her sit down on the bench inside. We sighed in relief. She peeled potatoes and popped string beans in the tree house a lot about this time of day, when the air had got a little cooler.

We figured she'd got back to normal.

Pretty soon the Spurgeons came sidling up the street. Miz Spurgeon was waddling along as usual, dragging a little cart piled high with old blankets and coats. She used these to make rag rugs to sell. Behind her came Mr. Spurgeon. He was skinny, short, had about five curls of gray hair on his head, and was bowlegged. He had thick arms and smoked a pipe. He looked just like Popeye.

The Spurgeons saw Aunt Daisy up in the tree house. They nodded to her and she nodded back. I know they nodded because Stella and I were in

Aunt Daisy's front room, watching and listening from the window. Then we heard Jervelle's big mouth get to going like a clapper in their kitchen.

"Look out now," said Stella.

In a flash we saw Miz Spurgeon march out to her front porch and sit down hard. She smoothed back her hair, crossed her arms, and glared up at Aunt Daisy. We could see three big noses pressed against the kitchen window, looking out.

"Your Matthew hit my baby Ervell lying in my Jervelle's arms," Miz Spurgeon said. "You ought to beat him good for doing it. I'm telling you this on account of I'm tired of your boy attacking my children."

"Well, you told," was all Aunt Daisy said. She kept right on peeling potatoes.

A good five minutes of silence must have passed after that. Miz Spurgeon stood up. "Well then, I want to know when *are* you gonna do something, 'cause it's obvious you ain't seen fit to do it yet." She'd put a snap to her voice.

We saw Aunt Daisy stand up, too. "When you pay taxes over here at three twelve Green Street, then you can tell me what to do." Aunt Daisy had a snap, crackle, *and* pop to her voice. "Your baboon-looking baby wouldn't have been hit if that big-eyed gal of yours and that goofy-looking other boy of yours hadn't started throwing insults and walnuts at Stella and Matthew."

Jervelle came out on the porch with Ervell still glued to her hip. "Momma, they started it," she said. She picked at a big white rag tied around Ervell from his waist all the way down to his toes. "We were tending to our own business when they started calling us names and throwing walnuts and hit poor Ervell up and down his leg."

"So there! You heard my daughter. This is one time too many. You better do something to him now, or I'll come do it to *you!*" Miz Spurgeon said.

When Aunt Daisy didn't move, Miz Spurgeon hunched up her shoulders, pulled down her lips, doubled up her fists, and stamped down her porch steps. Jervelle tried to do the same thing. They marched toward the tree house.

As soon as they put foot onto school property, Aunt Daisy jumped up. "You must be out of your mind!" she said. She grabbed up a potato, reared back her arm, and let that potato fly.

Miz Spurgeon leapt behind Jervelle. The potato hit the ground. Miz Spurgeon peeked out from behind Jervelle, and stuck out her tongue at Aunt Daisy.

But Jervelle lost her nerve. She ran back home,

leaving her momma with her mouth wide open.
Aunt Daisy cut loose with a potato, and BAM!
Popped Miz Spurgeon square in the chops. Miz
Spurgeon let out a whoop and then a hoot.

"Now you keep on coming on." Aunt Daisy
had a potato in one hand and a walnut in the
other. "Your gal's got more sense than you do.
Come on! I'll give you a walnut and potato fit you
won't ever forget!"

"Do it, Aunt Daisy!" Stella and I yelled.

Aunt Daisy fired again. One potato, two potato,
three potato, four sent ole Spurgeon flying back
to her front porch door.

Well, the dust settled. Aunt Daisy leaned back
against the side of the tree house with her hand
up to her chest. She caught her breath. After a
few minutes she came down the steps, picked her
potatoes up off the ground, and walked on home.

Aunt Daisy came inside into the front room and
sat down in her favorite rocking chair. She closed
her eyes and fanned herself with her wooden fan.
Stella and I sat as still as stone on the couch. Finally I nudged Stella. I figured it was safe for us
to go on home.

We stood up and tiptoed for the door.

"I got my eye on you, Matthew J. Cornelius
Carson," said Aunt Daisy. "And you, too, Estella

Elizabeth Carson. Send your souls to heaven and bring the rest to me."

Aunt Daisy paddled us with her fan. It didn't hurt, though, but she called our folks, too, and told them to paddle us again!

Jervelle, Nervell, Stella, and I had a couple more walnut fights after that, but I don't think Miz Spurgeon or Aunt Daisy found out about it. If they did, they kept it to themselves. At least Miz Spurgeon did. I don't think Aunt Daisy ever had to throw another walnut or potato at her, either.

NINE

The President's Wife

Ethel and I clapped and whistled over Aunt Daisy and the Walnut War.

"But don't you ever tell her that I told you," Daddy said. "She'd probably try to paddle me again."

Aunt Daisy being in the Women's Army Corps during World War II and driving ambulances made her as hard as nails on discipline and punishment. But she was also fair, he pointed out, and had a heart of gold.

I snapped my fingers. "That's why she wears that uniform and marches in parades, huh, because she was a soldier. But why does she march in a row all by herself?"

"Because that's the way Aunt Daisy wants it," he said. "Except one time she did march in a Veterans Day Parade here with a group of soldiers passing through who'd just come back from the Korean War. I was so proud of Aunt Daisy I didn't know what to do.

"There was even a picture of her marching in the old *Iowa Bystander* newspaper. That paper was located way up in Des Moines, Iowa! One of these days I'll have to tell you about that old *Iowa Bystander* newspaper. See, important folks like soldiers and such didn't come to Nutbrush too often, so we could only read about them. The *Bystander*, the old Kansas City *Call*, the St. Louis *Argus*—through those Black newspapers we were able to keep up with what was going on in the Black communities everywhere. And still do."

Daddy yawned. "But hey, the wife of a United States president came here one time."

"You mean, the one who has that dog that wrote a book?" asked Ethel.

"No, that's somebody else. I mean, Eleanor Roosevelt, wife of Franklin Roosevelt. She was probably the most famous of all the presidents' wives. She was a good friend to Dr. Mary McLeod Bethune, too, who was an internationally known educator and leader."

"Well, come on and tell us about when Mrs. Roosevelt came," I said.

On this particular Sunday afternoon, Elmo,

Delmo, Stella, and I were up here playing soccer, Daddy began. Delmo and I played against Stella and Elmo. I lined the ball up level with the edge of the old log cabin that used to set in the park area behind the school, near the highway. That was our goal line to defend.

The edge of the schoolhouse was the goal line for Stella and Elmo to defend. The object of the game was to beat up the other team and kick the ball over their goal line at the same time.

We couldn't play *too* rough, because if Stella got hurt it would be my fault. You know how that goes with little kids.

I kicked the ball hard over Stella's head to start us off. It landed just in front of my partner Delmo who guided it with quick little kicks toward the schoolhouse. Elmo, Stella's goalie, was back there waiting on him.

I followed behind, to be on hand to help and to protect our goal line at the same time.

Suddenly Elmo whizzed past Delmo and tripped him. Delmo went flat on his back while Elmo made off with the ball.

"Cheat! No fair!" I yelled. I flew into Elmo and tried to tangle up his feet with mine and get the ball away. But Elmo kicked the ball around to Stella, who galloped up the yard toward the log cabin.

I had almost caught up with her when Elmo banged into me and knocked me flat. I saw stars. By the time I got up, Delmo was hobbling after Stella. He caught up with her and stole the ball away. I raced to the log cabin. Just in time! Elmo stole the ball from Delmo and sliced it over to Stella. She cut loose with her best kick.

The ball popped up in the air and hit the roof of the cabin. I shot around to the other side. If I could catch it before it touched the ground, I could keep them from scoring. If I missed, they'd go ahead of us two to zip.

The ball rolled off the roof, hit a tree, and bounced over my head. I scrambled backwards, trying to catch it before it hit the ground.

"Stop!" everybody hollered, so I did.

And found myself in the middle of the street, with a big white car coming right at me!

Screech! The car stopped not two inches from me. I was so scared, I couldn't even breathe right. That car stopped so hard that it left tire marks on Highway 61 for a month afterwards. But better the road than on me.

"Kid?" A White man jumped out of the car and ran over to me. "Kid, are you okay?" He squatted down in front of me and patted me all over. "Didn't you see me?"

Sanity started to return to my brain. I managed to nod and shake my head.

"Matthew, Daddy told you not to get hit by no car, playing in the street," Stella yelled from the curb. "I'm tellin'!"

I didn't pay her any mind. I was listening to see if my heart had decided to finally slow down from going two hundred beats a second. A large lady wearing a little hat and a big fur stepped out of the car and walked quickly to me. "Child, have you been injured? Oh, I pray that it's not so."

She placed her hand under my chin and raised my head gently so she could look into my eyes. I had to look up into hers, too. She had kind eyes.

"I'm okay. I didn't get hit." My voice sounded squeaky.

"Well, that's a relief," the man said. "He's okay. It's getting late. We should get on to the college, Mrs. Roosevelt."

My mouth fell open, and my heart took off again. Did he say Mrs. Roosevelt? *The* Mrs. Eleanor Roosevelt? Herself? "Are you the real one? I mean, President Franklin Roosevelt's wife? Cross your heart and hope to die?"

"Yes, I'm Eleanor Roosevelt, but I don't hope to die, at least not anytime soon." She shook my hand. "And what is your name?"

I told her. "And these are my cousins Delmo and Elmo Bennett. They're twins. And this is my little sister Stella. She was the one who kicked the ball. I was trying to catch it so they couldn't score."

"But it went out-of-bounds," said Stella, "so we don't get a score, anyway. Hello."

"How do you do, Stella?" Mrs. Roosevelt went over to Stella and shook her hand. "You certainly are a good sport. That's the mark of a true athlete."

Stella's face lit up like a Christmas light.

Mrs. Roosevelt shook hands with Elmo and Delmo, too. Their mouths hung open so far that her car could have driven in through one and out through the other.

Mrs. Roosevelt asked me what grade I was in. I told her. "And our school, Frederick Douglass, is over there." I pointed to it. "Our teacher is Aunt Daisy Green and she lives over there." I pointed again. "She said you were going to give a speech at the college. That's where she is right now, waiting to see you. She's been talking about you all week. She said you knew Dr. Mary McLeod Bethune, too. I did a report on her one time."

"Matthew's got his mouth wide open and can't stop now," I heard Delmo whisper.

"Listen, Mrs. Roosevelt," I said, ignoring Delmo. I cleared my throat. "Dr. Mary McLeod

Bethune was a famous Black lady who told four U.S. presidents what to do. She started up a college in Florida by selling pies to workers. Aunt Daisy helped me look up stuff about her."

Mrs. Roosevelt nodded and smiled. "Your Aunt Daisy sounds like a wonderful teacher. Please tell her that I said thank you for her interest. And Dr. Bethune is a very good friend of mine. I want you to remember something very important. Dr. Bethune once said, 'Negro children have a right to whatever opportunities they show themselves capable of meeting.' I heartily agree. Please remember her words."

We said, "Yes, ma'am."

When she turned to go, I pulled on her fur piece. "Mrs. Roosevelt, I got a favor to ask." She raised her eyebrows. "When you see Dr. Bethune, would you tell her I got an *A* on my report?"

She smiled again. "Oh, splendid for you. Yes, I'll surely tell her." She got back into the car, and it rolled away.

Elmo, Delmo, Stella, and I watched until the car turned down a side street and disappeared. Then we started to scream and shout. "Man! We met President Franklin Roosevelt's wife!" Elmo shouted. "She shook this hand! I'm not gonna wash this hand for a week!"

Delmo did a little dance. "I'm not gonna wash this hand for a month!"

I waved my right hand in the air, then touched my chin. "And I'm not going to wash my hand or my face for a year!"

"That'll be more than what you wash them now," said smart-mouthed Stella.

Momma was standing on the front porch, waiting for us to get home. "The phone's been ringing off the hook," she said. "Everybody up and down the highway by the school saw Mrs. Roosevelt shake your hands." She hugged Stella.

"And saw you almost get hit by her car!" She patted me all over, then hugged me.

She made us tell her everything Mrs. Roosevelt had said. Dad came out and shook our hands, too. We had to repeat everything to him.

When word got around that we had met Eleanor Roosevelt, we had to get up in school and tell the other kids what happened. We had to do it in church the next Sunday. I even had to tell it at the gas station when I went by for a pop.

I hope Mrs. Roosevelt didn't forget to give my message to Dr. Bethune. I didn't forget hers.

TEN

The Gentle Giantess

"That was another good story, Daddy. But how come nothing like that happens here anymore?" I frowned. "There aren't any more floods. I've never even been in a walnut war. I never saw a turtle bite a dog. I've never even seen anybody famous."

"We saw Miss Missouri, Debbye Turner, when she came here," said Ethel.

"Yeah, but there were so many people around her that all I saw was her hand waving in the air."

Suddenly I remembered something. "Daddy, you know when you were talking about that shadow Aunt Daisy saw when she was at her clothesline? Maybe that was Ella Ewing."

"Who?" Ethel and Daddy said at the same time.

"Ella Ewing. Dr. Corbitt, our principal, told us about her. He said she was called the gentle giantess. She was eight feet four inches tall, and had hands as big as frying pans."

Ethel shook her head. "Margie can sure tell some whoppers, too, now, can't she, Uncle Matt?"

"Well, I *have* heard of somebody from around here who was supposed to be a giant, but I didn't put much stock to it. Miss Margie, tell us the story."

"Her name was Ella Ewing, and Dr. Corbitt said folks called her the world's tallest woman," I said. "She died when she was forty years old. She was born way back in 1872 somewhere south of La Grange."

Ethel raised her hand.

I stopped. "What, girl?"

"What's a La Grange?" she asked.

Daddy pointed in the direction of Highway 61. "It's a town. You keep straight on that road a few miles and you'll hit the town of La Grange. Go on, Margie."

"After she was born she moved to a town called Gorin, which is near La Grange, Ethel. She lived there the rest of her life. She had a house built just for her, with ten-foot-tall ceilings. She went all round the world and was even with a circus. Her hands were so large that a midget could stand in them."

"I bet she felt awful, being so big. I bet every-

body pointed and laughed at her," Ethel said. "I'da stayed home forever, right down in the basement, and let nobody ever see me."

"But Dr. Corbitt said Miss Ella Ewing never thought of herself as a freak or weird or anything." I remembered some more. "He said Ella's parents told her always to believe that she was beautiful inside. But yeah, it probably was hard for her. She was probably six foot tall when she was still a little kid. He said she was always friendly, loved to travel, and turned her liability into an asset. And that's all I remember."

Daddy patted me on the back. "You did a good job. When I heard of this woman, I hadn't really believed she was real, but you sure opened my eyes. See, you do have a story to tell. And remember that time Alberta tried to teach you how to ride your new bike by having you ride it down that hill on the first day?"

"Yeah, that was funny," I said. Well, it was now, but it sure wasn't then.

"Was I here when she did that?" Ethel asked.

"No, that was way before you came," he said. "She must have skinned up everything but her eyeballs. Margie, remember when you ate up Alberta's Christmas candy with your devilish self, and then helped her look two days for it?"

I crossed my legs and folded my arms. I wished he hadn't told that one. I didn't want to give Ethel ideas.

"I wasn't around here for that, either, I bet," said Ethel. She rested her chin on her hands and thumped her elbows down on her knees. I heard her sigh real hard.

I wondered what was wrong with her.

ELEVEN

Ethel's Story

The fire was starting to burn down again and we were out of crackers. Maybe Daddy was right. I guess if I thought hard, I could think about all kinds of stuff that happened. Telling about Ella Ewing to Daddy and Ethel was as much fun as watching TV. Hearing Daddy's stories was fun, too. Boy, it sure wasn't a boring night anymore!

"Well, ladies, I'm about storied out for tonight," said Daddy. He looked at his watch. "Hey, we've only been out here two hours. Seems like we've been out here for a hundred years and went all around the world. That's what storytelling can do for you. It can make you feel better for sure."

Daddy yawned. "Time for me to go to bed. You, too."

Ethel clacked her sandals against the step and poked out her lip. "I got a story, too."

"Oh, another country heard from," said Daddy. "Okay, you can wrap it up. Tell us a story."

Ethel twisted and squirmed. "Wait a minute." She stuck her finger in her mouth.

"You don't have a story," I said, and stood up. "C'mon, girl, let's go."

"Yes, I do!" She twisted and squirmed some more. Then she got real still. "Okay. Now. Once upon a time—"

"You don't start out these kinds of stories that way," I told her.

"Margie, she can start it any way she wants," Daddy said. "Go ahead, Ethel."

Once upon a time there was this little girl and she had a momma who loved her very, very much, Ethel began. They lived in a big fancy house. They never got cold at night. The little girl had lots of money, lots of clothes, lots of toys. She had all the pizzas, hamburgers, hot dogs, ice cream, French fries, and spaghetti and meatballs she wanted. She had her own color TV and her own phone and her own bathroom. Her momma was pretty, too, and drove a big fine car.

One day the momma told the little girl she had to go away for just a very little while. She promised that she'd be right back. The little girl said okay. She sat down and watched some TV. She talked on the phone to some of her friends, and did other stuff while she waited.

But when her momma didn't come back like she said, the little girl figured something awful had happened to her—like she got kidnapped! Yeah, that was it. Spies crept up behind her momma. They threw a blanket over her head, then they stuffed her in a sack.

They put her in a truck and they rode for a long time. Then they took her out of the truck and put her on a plane, and they flew way up in the air. Then they took her off the plane and put her in a submarine. It dived down, deep, deep, deep.

Finally the submarine came up to the top by a desert island. The kidnappers left the momma on the island with only stale bread, dried-up bologna, sauerkraut, and dirty water. They didn't even leave her any mayonnaise or mustard.

Meanwhile, the little girl still waited. She was lonely something awful for her momma. One day the little girl met a lady who asked her if she would like to come home and live with her till her momma came back. She said okay.

She left a note so her momma would know

where she was. The little girl went off and lived with the lady and her family. They were very nice. The lady had a nice husband and two nice daughters.

But she still missed her momma.

Her momma missed her, too. One day a sea serpent swam by the island.

"Hey, Mr. Sea Serpent," the momma hollered, and waved her arms.

The sea serpent came up on the land. "What's happening?" the sea serpent said.

"How much will it cost for you to take me back home?" the momma asked.

"Nothing, if you don't mind going to China first," the sea serpent said. "I have some very important appointments there. I can drop you off on the way back."

The momma said okay, and away they went. So one of these days the sea serpent is going to bring the momma back to the little girl, Ethel said. And when they get back together, they're gonna live happily ever after.

Ethel stopped talking. When we didn't say anything, she added, "The end."

"Gee, Ethel, you can tell a good one, too," I said. I felt sorry for the girl. The story sounded familiar, too. "Did you get that out of a book?"

"No, I made it up, but it's true, kind of."

"How can a story be true and be made up, too?" I asked.

"Margie, this is Ethel's story," Daddy said real soft. He put his arm around her. "That was a very important story, honey. Did the little girl understand that her new family loved her very much, too?"

"Yeah, she knows." She rested her chin back on her hands. "She just wants to see her momma. She doesn't know if her momma was really kidnapped, though. She made up that part so she could feel better, like you said."

"Well, I hope that little girl keeps remembering her mother, because maybe her mother will come back," said Daddy. "And I also hope that the little girl understands that her new family loves her, too, no matter what."

"Yeah, she does," said Ethel. She grinned a little at him. "I forgot to put that part in."

It hit me just then that Ethel was talking about herself! Her mother had been gone for three years now. Nobody knew where she was. If my mom hadn't let Ethel stay with us, she would have had to go to a children's shelter or to a foster home.

I bet Ethel never had anybody around to tell

her stories before she moved in with us, either. 'Course, I wasn't too hot on Ethel being around in the beginning, but I'm used to her now.

I guess she added that stuff about living in a fancy house and having lots of money to disguise who she was really describing.

Something else hit me. Ethel had put *me* in her story. I was one of the two nice daughters in there. I'd never been in anybody's story before, not even in Daddy's tonight.

Ethel's story wasn't in the past, either, like Daddy's stories were. Boy, that really got me thinking and planning. It also made me like Ethel a little more, too.

"Hey, everybody had a story to tell," I told Daddy. "Ethel, you're a pretty good storyteller," I told her. "Ethel, tomorrow let's write your story down. We can draw pictures. We can draw some of us sitting in front of Douglass School."

Ethel grinned. "And that shadow chasing Aunt Daisy."

I also planned to help her draw a picture of a kid in bed, wetting it up.

With a stick, Daddy dragged the rag-fire tub over to the ditch, which was filled with muddy water. He shoved the tub into the ditch. The hot coals steamed and fizzed when they hit the water. "We'll just leave the tub here till tomorrow, after it cools off. Nobody'll bother it," he said.

"Uncle Matt, is this the ditch where Smokey and that turtle went round and round?" Ethel asked. She kicked the tall weeds at the edge of the ditch. "Might be a big ole turtle around here now."

"We found a big ole long snake in there one time, too," he said. Ethel jumped back.

We walked back through the dark to our house, holding Daddy's hands. I didn't feel scared at all. Everything seemed normal again. Daddy turned on the TV set to a baseball game and lay down on the couch. Ethel and I went to our bedroom. We changed into T-shirts, cut off the lights, and fell on our bed. It was almost eleven o'clock.

"When's Alberta and Momma Luvenia coming back?" Ethel asked.

I told her that I didn't know. "They might have decided to stay over. I really liked your story. And don't worry about your momma. She's gonna come back home."

"Okay," said Ethel.

We lay there for a little while. Far off in the distance I heard a train whistle blow. I couldn't help myself. "Hear that? That's the sound of a giant vampire bat," I whispered in Ethel's ear.

"Don't even try it," Ethel replied. "I know a train whistle when I hear it."

"Okay. But I did see something just then that looked like the shadow Aunt Daisy saw," I went on, "right by the window."

"I'm not scared of nothing but Freddy Krueger," Ethel said, "so hang it up, Margie." She put her pillow over her head.

Just then the walnut tree branches scratched at our window. "The shadow!" I pounced on Ethel and started to tickle her.

Ethel shrieked. She pushed me off her, and ran into the living room where Daddy was.

"And she said the shadow was in our room," I heard her say, "and she was tickling me so bad, I almost wet up the bed."

"But you didn't," I heard Daddy say. "You're getting better. Let me tell you this story real quick about something that happened to me and almost made me wet *my* pants—and I was grown at the time!"

I crept to the doorway and peeked in. Ethel had her fingers up in front of her face and was looking through them. "Oh, I know this story is gonna be awful. I'm scared. No, I'm not. Uncle Matt, make it with monsters, okay? But no slime. And put something in about volcanoes erupting, and ghosts, and Smokey, okay?"

"Maybe we can make one up and tell it together," Daddy said.

Now that really did sound like fun. I slipped into the room. "Hi, you guys. Can I tell some of it, too?"

A Note from the Author

Some of the events that occurred in the mythical town of Nutbrush, Missouri, and at Douglass School are drawn from the actual history of the tiny Mississippi River town of Canton, Missouri, population twenty-five hundred, and its real one-room Lincoln "Colored" School. I was born in Canton, and spent thirteen of my childhood years there, where I grew to love rag fires, writing, the Mississippi River, stories, and storytelling.

Most of the stories that Matthew J. Cornelius Carson tells his daughter Margie and niece Ethel are based on my own actual experiences, or on stories I heard and greatly embellished.

The accounts of Ella Ewing, the "gentle giantess," are true, according to news stories in the Canton *Press-News Journal*. She was a celebrity in her time. *The Guinness Book of Records* questions whether Ella Ewing was actually as tall as accounts of the time declared.

Stateswoman and first lady Mrs. Eleanor Roosevelt visited Canton October 4, 1953, and spoke at Canton's Culver-Stockton College Centennial Program as part of her work with the American Association for the United Nations.

Floods periodically inundated portions of Canton from the time of its founding in 1830 until the mid-1950s, and gave rise to disaster and river stories. A particularly cherished true story about Canton and its floods involves the rivalry between Canton and the village of Tully, located at one time just north of Canton. The two little towns were fiercely competitive in their dealings with each other, until a major flood in the 1850s washed tiny Tully away.

Lincoln School was flooded almost yearly by the Mississippi River which ran three blocks east of it. The school's "Historic Inventory" report filed at the State of Missouri's State Historical Survey and Planning Office in Jefferson City relates that "the floor was damaged and replaced many times, finally with concrete."

To my knowledge, no Lincoln children experienced the adventures that the character Matthew describes in the flood incident and in the others. That a Chihuahua could have entered Lincoln School disguised as a possum also is unlikely.

As I grew up in Canton, my grandmother, the late Mrs. Corinne Johnson, told me stories of all kinds, including stories of her own childhood. Some of them were actually told around a small fire at our house, usually burning in a small tin bucket on the sidewalk, to ward off mosquitoes on hot summer nights.

When I was nine or ten years old, she told me the story of the casket and the dead man. It wasn't until I became an adult and began to study folklore that I discovered how widespread—and popular—that particular story is. I had thought it had happened in Canton. The casket story was a companion story to another traditional tale Grandmother told to me. This story, which is also a staple in folklore, traditionally involves a man or woman who through some circumstance of health or devilishness falls into a catatonic state and is buried alive.

Second Baptist Church of Canton, where I was a member, was founded in 1895 and closed its doors in 1989. It was the model for Nubia Missionary Baptist Church both in this book and in its companion, *Just an Overnight Guest*. As of this writing, the building, a white brick structure that I had thought was enormous when I was a child, is still standing. Accounts in the *Canton Sesquicentennial Book, 1830-1980,* show that the building where Second Baptist was located was built in 1834.

Early written newspaper and historical accounts of educational opportunities for Black youth in Canton prior to the construction of Lincoln show that various small buildings, including one behind the African Methodist Episcopal Church (as well as the church itself), were used as schools during the 1860s and 1870s.

Lincoln School is only one of a very few nineteenth-century midwestern one-room schools still standing. It was built of brick in 1880 at a cost of seven hundred dollars. Its dimensions were forty-two feet by twenty-four feet. Prof. M. L. Clay was hired at a "salary of thirty-five dollars a month," followed by Mr. Charles W. Lear. From 1881 until 1955 Lincoln was used to educate hundreds of area African-American children in accordance with the state's 1866 laws mandating public education for White and Black children on a racially "separate but equal" basis.

During that time, Mr. Lear taught at Lincoln a total of thirty-two years. Black students wishing to continue their schooling were bused some forty miles each way to Hannibal, Missouri, to attend its Black high school.

But after the United States Supreme Court outlawed racial segregation in the schools May 17, 1954, Canton's African-American high school students in September of that year peacefully integrated the town's White system. Lincoln children entered the system the following fall, in September of 1955. My first grade was completed during Lincoln's last year, September 1954–May 1955.

My first-grade teacher was Mrs. Bertie Nickerson.

She was *not*, however, the prototype for the character Aunt Daisy Green, who is a completely fictional character.

Through the dedicated efforts of the late historian Colman Winn, archivist at Culver-Stockton College, the school was placed on the National Register of Historic Places in 1983. Efforts are underway for the school's restoration. Winn's research, and mine at the Lewis County Historical Society and the Canton Public Library, along with newspapers, historical accounts, and conversations with long-time Canton residents such as Mrs. Grace Pleasant, all provided me with ample information.

The African Methodist Episcopal Church in Nutbrush is drawn from the one located in Canton. As of this writing, the old church is still standing, though it has been closed for many years. There have been rumors that it may be used for a Confederate museum.

Lincoln School remains a testament to the determination of Canton's Black residents to educate their children regardless of the cost; to Canton's Whites who worked to help make that a reality; and to rural education.

Lincoln, and other schools like it, offered intimacy, sincerity, and commitment by its teachers, the expectation of a quality education in a supportive atmosphere, positive role models, and support from the community.

Help is needed to preserve Lincoln School and its rich history. Persons wishing more information about the Lincoln School Historic Preservation Project and about Canton should write to the Canton Chamber of Commerce, Canton, Missouri 63435.

Eleanora E. Tate
Myrtle Beach, South Carolina
December 1991

Witty and Sassy, the Voice of Narrator Zambia Brown Will Instantly Grab Your Attention!

0-440-41209-9

Life seems boring for twelve-year old Zambia, who lives in the country with her aunt, uncle, and cousin. When her father opens up a nightclub down the road, she dreams of a new life sharing his flashy cars, clothes, and cash. But the club is attracting the wrong kind of people. Will the town and Zambia ever feel safe again?

Available from Yearling Books